Charlie's Magical Journey to Zifferland

by Charles Elias

Special thanks to family and friends
for their support and encouragement.

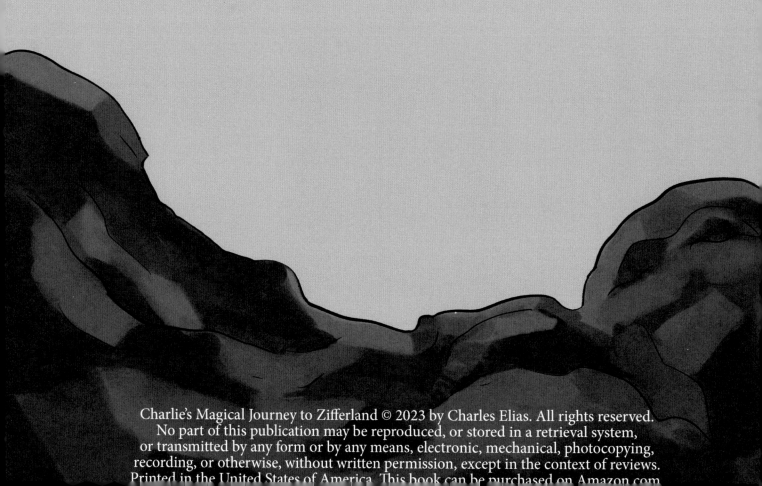

Charlie's Magical Journey to Zifferland

1
Hobart Explains Zifferland

One cool morning as the sun was rising over the horizon, Charlie and his talking horse, Fred, said good-bye to his family and set out for a new adventure. Charlie was the apprentice of Hobart the Wizard and had powers with his magic wand. Where would he use his magic next?

Charlie's new adventure would be a trip into the mountains with Fred. Fred was gifted with special magical powers to talk. Hobart was sending Charlie on an adventure to find his three brothers who had been cursed by the wicked Wizard that had turned his brothers into dwarf goats living up in the cursed mountains of Zifferland. Their names were Zoco, Zeb, and Zeek – funny names for three silly little wizards. Hobart had told Charlie about this land and instructed him to travel with Fred, and Ziggy the mouse. Charlie, Ziggy, and Fred were sent by Hobart to save his brothers from their curse.

Hobart stated, "In this obscure realm, things will be different on the other side of the magical forest." Hobart instructed Charlie to travel through the forest until he met with Ziggy the mouse. There in the forest by a very large Redwood tree that towered extremely high, Ziggy would meet them and show Charlie the way through the other side of the redwood tree. This would bring Ziggy and Charlie together. When Charlie came out of the tree with Fred, they would be in Zifferland. This is a place where he would face many strange and mysterious animals, fairies, and elves who would guide him through the lands. Hobart said that he wouldn't be able to pass through that dimension in time but would be with Charlie in spirit. "The elves and my three brothers, Zoco, Zeb, and Zeek, will be there to help you and your friends. They will be able to give you some magical items to help guide you through the magical forest. Use those items to guide you home safely," said Hobart.

2
Charlie and Fred Set Out to Zifferland

Charlie remembered what Hobart had told him. Hobart said his brothers were always causing trouble, which landed them into the cursed mountain where they were cursed by a wicked wizard. Hobart explained to Charlie that the goats were his brothers, and they could talk as goats. Nevertheless, they had magical powers and did have a good knowledge of the kingdom that Charlie was traveling through. The wizards could guide him through the mountains of Zifferland.

The Grand Wizard of Zifferland was displeased by the three wizards using their magic unwisely. They wanted to rule the kingdom of Zifferland, but by using their magic unwisely this became a curse which placed them in the isolated mountains. Hopefully this would teach them to be humbler.

Charlie and Fred set out and rode all day and night over rough terrain. Finally, on the third cool night, they decided to bed down and rest near a large tree in the dark. Charlie and Fred were tired and fell fast asleep with only one red blanket that one of them could use. The two of them were chilled that night. Charlie decided to use the red blanket to cover Fred. Charlie waved his wand and said, "blue blanket," which created a blue blanket for himself. The next morning, Charlie was awakened by the sunlight. Black ravens were flying by, and at the bottom of the tree was Ziggy the mouse screaming.

"Help!" shouted Ziggy. "The ravens are trying to eat me!"

Charlie and Fred jumped up. Charlie picked up the mouse and placed him in his front pocket. "There, Ziggy. You're safe now," said Charlie.

Ziggy calmed down and replied, "Hi, guys. Thank you for saving me. Glad you finally got here okay." Charlie and Fred were happy to see their friend Ziggy. "You slept at the bottom of the Redwood tree," Ziggy stated. "We will go through the entrance hole in the redwood tree and on the other side we will be in Zifferland."

"Okay!" Charlie exclaimed. Thankfully Fred could fit through the tree with a little help from Charlie's magic wand!

3
The Other Side of the Redwood Tree

Charlie and Fred walked out bravely with Ziggy in Charlie's shirt pocket. Fred exclaimed, "Charlie, we are in Zifferland!" Charlie had forgotten Fred could speak. Fred had been quiet most of the time along their journey.

The group noticed a brilliant blue sky and birds flying among the beautiful, colorful flowers. Waterfalls were abundant and in the distance. Charlie could see mountains and rivers around the bend. Fred heard strange sounds behind the colorful flowers. It sounded like many hummingbirds flying about. A small fairy appeared and then disappeared. Charlie and Ziggy heard the strange humming of fairies. They were all around him, giggling. They seemed to be happy fairies.

Suddenly all of the fairies disappeared except one. She flew in front of Fred and said, "My name is Carrisa! Welcome to the magical land of Zifferland."

"Charlie and I are with our friend Ziggy the mouse. We are looking for Hobart's brothers, who live high up in the mountains," replied Fred.

"They have been cursed to be dwarf mountain goats by the wicked Grand Wizard," said Charlie.

"Have you seen the wizards?" asked Fred.

"We are here to help them to be freed from their curse," added Charlie.

The pixie fairy laughed at the silly group and said, "You will meet my sister, Aurora. She can guide you and give you more information. If you can find the magic crystals and sprinkle them on Hobart's brothers' heads, they will return to the wizards they were and be free them from their curse."

Charlie smiled, knowing that is why he came to the Zifferland. The fairy went off flying through the forest. Suddenly behind a tree appeared a pretty fairy named Aurora.

"Hello," said Aurora. "My sister Carrisa said you needed some help. I am here to help you find Noggleburt. He is an elf that lives far in the forest beyond the waterfall. He can help you find your three wizard friends. Carrisa mentioned that you need the blue Safire, fairy crystals to return your wizard friends back

from their curse. Noggleburt has better knowledge of that part of the woods. I will take all of you to his home if you can keep up with me." Aurora told Charlie and his friends where the hiding place was for the fairies' blue Safire crystals. "Under the red crystal waterfall, you will find the blue Safire crystals, near the center of the cave," said Aurora. Then she took off flying through the woods in a puff. Running as fast as they could, Charlie, Fred, and Ziggy tried to keep up with her on their way to Noggleburt's home.

4
Searching for Noggleburt the Elf

Charlie traveled through the forest on Fred's back. Ziggy traveled in Charlie's front pocket. The fairy swooped though the branches as Fred moved along, trying to keep up with her. After running all that time, through the woods an opening appeared in the forest. There were colorful mushrooms everywhere. They were so large that they towered over Fred and Charlie's heads! Ziggy jumped out of Charlie's pocket and made an attempt to reach part of the mushroom on the top of Fred's head with his tiny hands. He had no luck so Fred gave it a try with his nose and a piece fell on the ground. Fred gave it a munch and soon realized that the mushroom tasted sweet like an apple. Charlie tried some too, then Ziggy had a piece. They all sat around eating large purple pieces of the mushroom that had fallen to the ground.

Suddenly a little groundhog appeared and said, "Hey! Are you eating pieces of my mushrooms?" With laugher, he realized there was plenty of the pieces for everyone. "Save some for me"! I am Walter the forest guide. I have been informed by Aurora to help you find Noggleburt the elf." Walter was a small groundhog with a deep voice.

"I can wave my wand and make you a bigger groundhog and then you will be able to lead Fred and me through the dense forest!" exclaimed Charlie. With one wave of Charlie's wand and the command, "Grow bigger," the groundhog shook his head then became as tall as a human. He wore blue suspenders and a brown scaly cap on his head.

The group then followed the groundhog through a cave and came out through the other side. When Charlie and Fred came out, they noticed there was a little cottage with a thatched roof in front of them. There was a marsh in front of the hills. They finally arrived at Noggleburt's house, which wasn't too far from the foothills of the mountains.

5
Noggleburt's Secret Mountain

Noggleburt, a small elf with a chubby nose and silly laugh, was welcoming to all when they were able to enter the cottage after Charlie did his magic, shrinking them all down to elf-like sizes.

"Hi, Noggleburt!" replied Charlie.

Noggleburt knew what Charlie and the gang was there for after speaking with Carrisa. "Tomorrow, I will give you the directions through the forest to your wizards' home."

Charlie, Fred, Walter, and Ziggy were all happy to be snuggled in their beds with blankets, sleeping near Noggleburt's fireplace. "We will be off tomorrow morning," Charlie said.

"To get through the forest we will need lots of sleep," replied Walter.

"Yes," said Charlie. "Don't forget, we need to find the Cave of Crystals and find the pouch that Aurora the fairy instructed us to find under the red crystal."

Noggleburt agreed, then climbed up a small wooden ladder into his bed. He was up in a double wooden bunk. His brother, Smort, slept below on the lower bunk bed. The next morning, Smort was out on a hunt, searching for edible mushrooms and giant blueberries for breakfast.

6
Journey to Wizard's Mountain

Early the next morning, Charlie had awoken with the sound of frogs chirping and burping in the marsh. "Ribbit, ribbit," said the chirping frogs. Suddenly he heard bang, bang, knock, knock. What was that loud noise at the door? Everyone woke up to that loud sound. It was Smort, a chubby little elf with a long red beard. What was that long purple thing hanging from his beard?

Noggleburt woke up and said, "Don't worry. That's my brother, Smort, at the door."

Smort was dragging in a large net with the largest blueberries anyone had ever seen. A purple frog jumped off Smort's beard then jumped onto the floor and out the door toward the marsh.

Noggleburt made a great breakfast for his brother and the others: blueberry pancakes with mushrooms for dessert. As they sat across from the fireplace at a wooden table, they ate and laughed. What a wonderful morning! They would be heading out into the mountains to search for Zoco, Zeb, and Zeek soon. Noggleburt had instructed Charlie and his friends how to use his map.

"In the cave you will find the blue crystal near the waterfall. After leaving the cave you will find a hole outside the exit. With the pouch in hand, you must slide down the hole through the to the other side of the mountain. The mountain is named after the wizards. It's called Mount Wizard," informed Noggleburt.

Charlie, Fred, Walter, and Ziggy left Noggleburt's home. After leaving the cottage, they returned to their original sizes with the help of Charlie waving his magic wand.

Along the way, Ziggy fell asleep in Charlie's pocket while Fred marched on. There were lots of things to see like flowers and trees with many rivers.

All of a sudden, behind a branch on the tree, a little head popped out. It was Aurora. "Hi, everyone!" shouted Aurora. She was just in time to show Charlie and his friends the way to Mount Wizard. "Come this way," she said with a smile.

After greeting her, the group followed Aurora. She said, "We must pass through the orchard of living trees." Up ahead there were 14 trees lined up in a long row. The trees would not let them pass through. The first tree in the row was named Morris. He said, "No passers along this passage."

Charlie took out his magic wand and said, "Ground trees unite and hold hands." With a pass of his wand, all the trees held their branches together like holding hands and made a bridge like path for the gang. They walked over their branches, which felt slippery. Fred the horse slipped but they were okay.

Then Josh, the large tree, said, "Be careful boys."

Ziggy had no problem in Charlie's cushioned pocket. Walter just skipped along the trail. Before long, they all fell asleep in a pile of grass on the side of the trail. Nighttime felt very peaceful.

By morning the sunrise felt warm. The group wanted to move on towards Wizards Mountain.

7
Into the Cave of Crystals

After waking up and having a mushroom breakfast, Charlie knew it was just a walk down the hill to the cave entrance, but the fairies had mentioned it may not be so easy to get the magic crystals. There it was: the entrance of the cave with a river flowing through it.

"We need a raft," said Charlie. The others agreed. With a wave of Charlie's magic wand Charlie said, "Build me a raft for my friends." Branches of trees flew into the air and magically weaved themselves together to make the perfect raft and laid itself right next to the river. "Let's go!" said Charlie.

"Can't wait to get the blue Safire Crystal," said Fred.

Walter, Fred, and Ziggy jumped up onto the raft. Charlie gave the raft a push into the river before leaping on it himself, and off they went down the river into the mouth of the cave. There were many different colors of crystals on the wall of the cave. Some were orange some purple, some red, and some green. Where would the blue crystal be? It had the magic to turn Hobart's brothers into normal wizards.

Aurora had mentioned going to the middle of the cave to find the mysterious magic crystal. There were three holes in the cave's walls that looked like three passages to the middle of the cave.

Suddenly a serpent popped its head up and said, "Hi, I am Amy, the friendly serpent! I can take you to the magical blue crystal." Amy guided the raft toward the middle of the cave. There were red crystals above the river on the ceiling. Below the boat was the blue magical Safire crystal that Charlie and his friends needed. Charlie jumped into the cold river and swam to the bottom where he saw the blue crystal glimmering then grabbed the crystal he needed. After stuffing it under his shirt, he swam to the surface then onto his raft and held the crystal in the air. Walter, Fred, and Ziggy were happy to finally get what they came for, the magic crystal. They thanked Amy for her service and started on their way out of Wizards Mountain to find the three wizards.

8
The Long Climb to Save Zoco, Zeb and Zeek

They were on their way to Wizards Mountain. The mountain was at the end of the river they had traveled down. There it was: the mountain they all were looking for. Soon the curse would be over. Charlie, Fred, Walter, and Ziggy had traveled and climbed over many rocks and passed by many trees along the way. They looked in a cave on the mountain, but there were no goats.

Suddenly a goat appeared behind a rock and said to Fred and the group, "I was told you were sent by my brother Hobart to save us."

On the journey, Charlie had carried the blue crystal in his pocket. It suddenly began to feel warm; as he removed the rock, it glowed. Charlie crumbled the rock and sprinkled the blue magic dust over the goat's head. The goats stood up on their hind legs then the mountain shook. The wizards were now back and looked like the wizards they were before they were cursed by the wicked Grand Wizard. They thanked Charlie, Fred, Walter, and Ziggy.

Their long journey was a happy adventure and coming to an end. The three knew Hobart would be happy that his brothers were safe and the wizards could return home. The wizards rewarded the group by sending them back to the entrance near the redwood tree where they had started their journey. As they walked home, they realized they had a great adventure together and made great friendships throughout the land of Zifferland.

Meet
Charles Elias

Author Charles Elias resides in Portsmouth, NH,
in New England.

Charles enjoys writing stories for children
with a lesson involved, such as caring for others!

His stories include:
Charlie Works at the Grocery Store
Charlie's Spooky Halloween
Charlie Meets Hobart the Wizard #1
Charlie's Magical Journey to Zifferland #2